MINECRAFT

STICKER ADVENTURE
TREASURE HUNT

RANDOM HOUSE 🏠 NEW YORK

Published in the United States by Random House Children's Books, a division of Penguin Random House LLC, 1745 Broadway, New York, NY 10019, and in Canada by Penguin Random House Limited, Toronto.
Random House and the colophon are registered trademarks of Penguin Random House LLC.
First published in Great Britain 2022 by Farshore, an imprint of Harper Collins Publishers.
rhcbooks.com
minecraft.net
ISBN 978-0-593-57202-3
MANUFACTURED IN CHINA
10 9 8 7 6 5 4 3 2

ADVENTURE PACK

Alex and Steve are getting ready to go hunting for treasure, but before they set foot out of their base, they need to make sure they're properly equipped.

Read the clues below to help each of them fill their hotbar.

- Steve is going to need some ammo for his bow.

- Alex needs a weapon that can survive in lava.

- Steve needs a drink that'll cure status effects.

- Alex prefers a food she can place down and share with Steve.

- Steve is planning on some mining and will need a tool to help.

- Alex likes a tool that she can also wield as a weapon.

- Steve likes to know which direction he's traveling in.

- Alex likes to be prepared to travel across water.

ALL THAT GLISTERS

Alex spots an opening in the ground, which leads to a cave overflowing with ores.

Help them out by counting how many of each ore you can see in the cave.

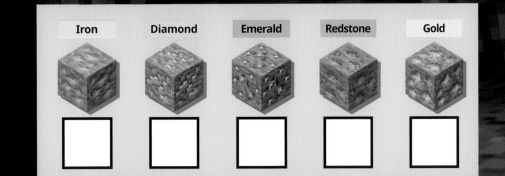

Iron	Diamond	Emerald	Redstone	Gold

FINISH

ABANDONED MINESHAFT

Alex and Steve have cleaned out the mine and are ready to take their haul back to their base. Steve finds an abandoned mineshaft that can take them back to the surface.

Use rail stickers to fix the route and lead them out.

START

MOB AMBUSH

Oh, dear! Hostile mobs have gathered to block the cave entrance and won't let Alex and Steve pass.

Place the missing mob stickers. Then match the mobs into pairs so the friends can deal with the beasts quickly.

A

B

C

1

2

3

D

4

5

E

VILLAGE UNDER SIEGE

As they emerge from the cave, Alex and Steve spot trouble in a nearby village. It's under attack by pillagers!

Add stickers to the scene to help Alex and Steve fight off the invaders.

FIND THE CARTOGRAPHER

The villagers celebrate as the pillagers are finally defeated! Alex and Steve have a taste for adventure now, and they've heard rumors of a cartographer who could send them on their next epic quest.

Place the villager stickers on their silhouettes. Then use the clues below to find out which one is the cartographer.

A

D

B

C

E

CLUES: THE CARTOGRAPHER HAS...

ANSWER:

Red sleeves ■ No hat ■ A green laurel around his head ■ Something gold over his eye

ADVENTURE PACK P2

ABANDONED MINESHAFT P4

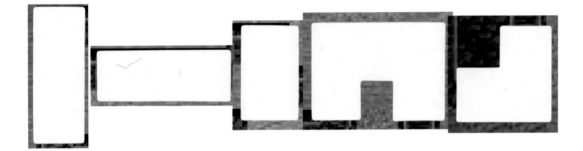

MOB AMBUSH P5

MAP TRADE

The heroes have tracked down the cartographer, who has a map for buried treasure.

Use the trades below to figure out how many emeralds each item costs. Then fill in the cost boxes. Use the costs to calculate the final sum and discover how many emeralds the map will cost.

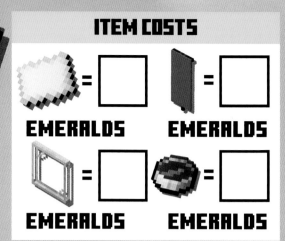

ITEM COSTS

[ ] EMERALDS   [ ] EMERALDS

[ ] EMERALDS   [ ] EMERALDS

TRADES

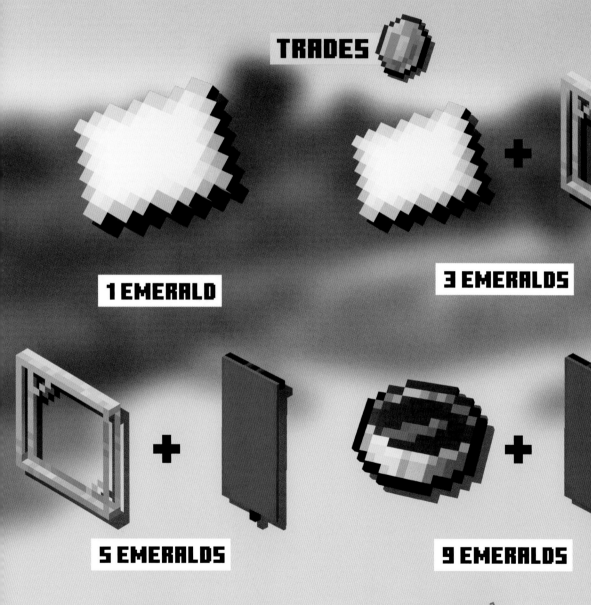

1 EMERALD

3 EMERALDS

5 EMERALDS

9 EMERALDS

HOW MANY EMERALDS DO YOU NEED? [ ]

1
2
3
4
5
6
7
8
9
10
11
12
13
14
15
16
17

X MARKS THE SPOT

Alex and Steve have finally gotten their hands on an ocean explorer map, which should lead them to buried treasure.

Can you follow the directions to the site of the treasure and place an X sticker to mark the spot?

START

North 4

East 7

South 3

East 2

North 5

West 3

North 2

East 7

South 9

West 10

South 3

West 3

South 1

East 16

North 3

East 6

North 8

West 6

North 4

East 2

TURTLE BEACH

To get the treasure, Alex and Steve are going to need to dive underwater. They'll need five scutes to craft a turtle shell so that they can breathe.

Follow each turtle to see which ones have left behind scutes on their beaches.

A

B

C

D

E

1

2

3

4

5

DOLPHIN'S GRACE

Now that they've gotten their turtle-shell helmets, the friends make their way out to the middle of the ocean, but they're surprised by dolphins along the way.

Can you spot seven differences between these two pictures?

THE DESCENT

When they get to the right spot on the map, Alex and Steve descend into the water, but it's hard to find their way in the dark.

Use your stickers to complete the grid. Then use the sequence to help them find their way to the treasure.

SEQUENCE

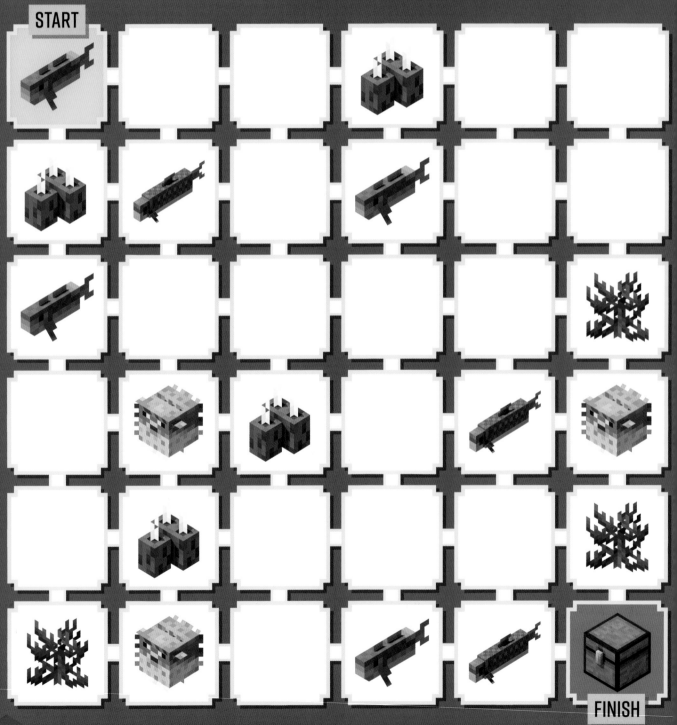

START

FINISH

14

BURIED TREASURE

Alex opens the buried treasure and finds dozens of cool items ... except it's so dark that she can't make out what they are.

Match each of the mysterious silhouettes to the correct item to help her out.

CRACKING THE CONDUIT

Steve and Alex study the mysterious blue orb they found — the heart of the sea. A nearby sign explains how to craft it into a conduit to unlock three mysterious effects, but the effects are written in an unusual language.

Use the key below to decipher each effect.

1

__ __ __ __ __ __

2

__ __ __ __ __

__ __ __ __ __

3

__ __ __ __ __ __

__ __ __ __ __ __ __ __ __

A	B	C	D	E	F	G	H	I	J	K	L	M	N	O	P	Q	R	S	T	U	V	W	X	Y	Z

FIND THE CARTOGRAPHER P8

THE DESCENT P14

BURIED TREASURE P15

GOLD COLLECTION P18

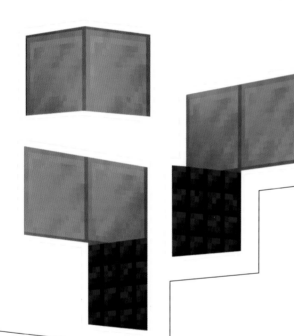

CONDUIT CONSTRUCTION P19

STICKERS FOR FUN!

EXPLORING THE OCEAN MONUMENT

Alex and Steve are about to head back to the surface when Steve spies an ocean monument.

Help them navigate the maze, avoiding the guardians, to find the monument's treasure room.

START

FINISH

GOLD COLLECTION

There doesn't seem to be anything in the treasure chamber, but Alex starts to mine the prismarine anyway. Suddenly, she hits the jackpot.

Use the stickers from the sticker sheet to complete the scene and see what she's found.

CONDUIT CONSTRUCTION

What was that sound? It looks like Steve and Alex aren't alone in the ocean monument.

Help them unlock the conduit's power by building the structure to house it so they can get ready for a fierce fight.

Find the block stickers on your sticker sheet and use the key at the bottom of the page to create the five layers you need to build the conduit structure.

LAYER 3

LAYER 2

LAYER 1

LAYER 5

LAYER 4

| PRISMARINE | | WATER | | CONDUIT |

BATTLE OF THE OCEAN MONUMENT

Alex and Steve built the conduit just in time, but they're ambushed by an elder guardian, guardians, and a bunch of drowned.

Use your stickers to complete the scene and help our heroes escape the ocean monument.

TRIDENT TROPHY

One of those drowned dropped a cool trident, so Alex and Steve are trying out some new moves.

Can you figure out the next move in each sequence?

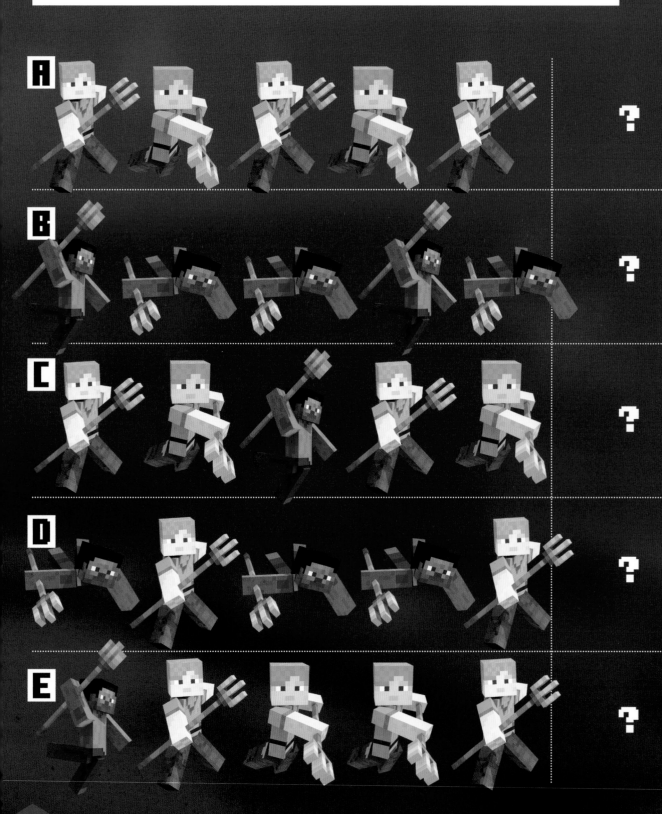

HERO CREDENTIALS

Alex and Steve have finally returned home with their haul of treasure and excitedly recap their favorite of the adventure.

How much of the adventure do you remember? See how many of these questions you can answer correctly.

1 Which transport did Alex and Steve take out of the abandoned mineshaft?

2 What's the name of the mob group that attacks villages?

3 Which villager will trade a map with you?

4 What's the name of the buff that a dolphin can give you?

5 Which rare item do you use to craft a conduit?

6 Which block should you use to build the structure that holds a conduit?

7 Which two one-eyed mobs protect the ocean monument?

8 What weapon does the drowned mob sometimes drop when it's defeated?

ANSWERS

P2 - Adventure Pack:

STEVE :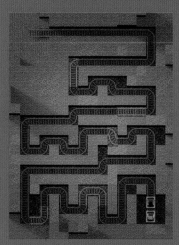

ALEX:

P3 - All That Glisters:
Iron: 5, Diamond: 1, Emerald: 1,
Redstone: 2, Gold: 2

P4 - Abandoned Mineshaft:

P5 - Mob Ambush:
A-3, B-2, C-5, D-1, E-4

P8 - Find The Cartographer:
The cartographer is villager D.

P9 - Map Trade:
You need 20 emeralds to buy the
buried treasure map.

PP10-11 - X Marks the Spot

P12 - Turtle Beach:
Turtles A and C have left behind a
scute on their beaches.

P13 - Dolphin's Grace:

P14 - The Descent:

P15 - Buried Treasure:
A-5, B-6, C-1, D-7, E-3, F-4, G-2

P16 - Cracking the Conduit:
1: HASTE, 2: NIGHT VISION,
3: WATER BREATHING

P17 - Exploring the Ocean Monument:

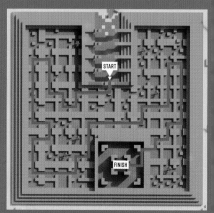

P22 - Trident Trophy:

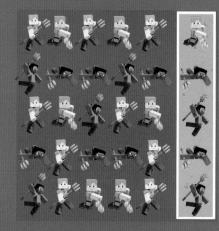

P23 - Hero Credentials:
1: minecart, 2: pillagers;
3: cartographer, 4: dolphin's grace,
5: heart of the sea, 6: prismarine,
7: guardians and elder guardians;
8: trident

TRIDENT TROPHY P22

STICKERS FOR FUN!

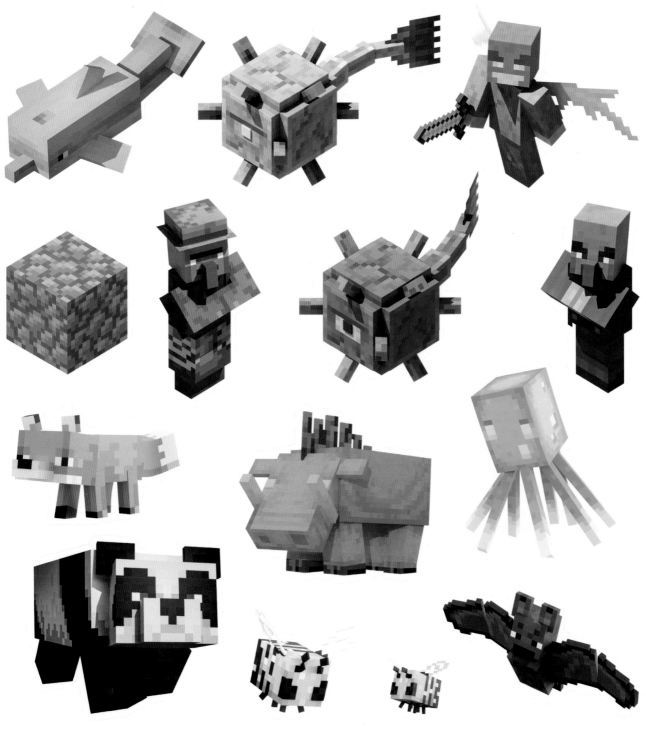